Writing Builders

Bridget and Bo Build a
BLOG

by Amanda StJohn
illustrated by Katie McDee

Content Consultant
Jan Lacina, Ph.D.
College of Education
Texas Christian University

NORWOOD HOUSE ⬛ PRESS
CHICAGO, ILLINOIS

Norwood House Press
P.O. Box 316598
Chicago, Illinois 60631
For information regarding Norwood House Press, please visit
our website at:
www.norwoodhousepress.com or call 866-565-2900

Editor: Melissa York
Designer: Becky Daum
Project Management: Red Line Editorial

Library of Congress Cataloging-in-Publication Data
StJohn, Amanda, 1982-
  Bridget and Bo build a blog / by Amanda St. John ; illustrated
by Katie McDee.
      p. cm. -- (Writing builders)
  Includes bibliographical references.
  Summary: "While on vacation, Bo learns how to write a blog.
When he comes back home he teaches his friend Bridget how
to start and maintain one"--Provided by publisher.
  ISBN-13: 978-1-59953-507-4 (library ed. : alk. paper)
  ISBN-10: 1-59953-507-6 (library ed. : alk. paper)
  ISBN-13: 978-1-60357-387-0 (e-book : alk. paper)
  ISBN-10: 1-60357-387-9 (e-book : alk. paper) 1. Online
authorship--Juvenile literature. 2. Language arts (Elementary)
I. McDee, Katie, ill. II. Title.
  PN171.O55S75 2012
  808--dc23
                              2011039361

Manufactured in the United States of America in North
Mankato, Minnesota.
195N—012012

Words in **black bold** are defined in the glossary.

I Love to Blog!

Last month I went to England with my family to visit my grandmother. England was a great place, but I missed my friends. Usually I do everything with my friends. Sometimes, I felt very lonely.

My mom didn't want me to feel homesick. Together we created a blog—that means 'weblog,' a kind of journal you share online. A blog is all about how you see the world. Each day I posted news and photos from my adventures. My American friends read my blog and posted comments on it like, "we miss you" or "you're lucky to see London!"

My best friend is Bridget. She read my blog while I was gone. Now that I'm home, she told me she wants a blog like mine. We'll tell all of our friends about our blogs. Maybe they'll start blogs too!

By Bo, age 9

"Are you ready to b-l-o-g?" called Bo as Bridget arrived at his house.

"Ready!" replied Bridget. "My dad helped me join a blog website. We created my user name and password. But you have to help me write something to . . . to . . ."

". . . to post," helped Bo. "When you put new writing on your blog, it's called posting."

"Posting," repeated Bridget. "Got it."

Bridget and Bo went to the computer. They logged in to the blog website and admired Bridget's blog space. It had a light gold text box with dark green type. The text box was framed with drawings of trees.

"Cool colors," congratulated Bo.

"Thanks!" said Bridget. "My dad helped me choose a free design from the blog website. He called it a **template**."

"So, what's your subject?" asked Bo.

"I can't decide," said Bridget, frowning.

Bo thought for a moment. "Well, I love learning about England and Europe even when I'm not there, so that's what I picked. What do you think about every day?"

Just then Mrs. Grant, Bo's mom, came into the room. "I know what Bridget thinks about," she said, smiling. "Birds."

Bridget's eyes lit up. "That's true. I know more about birds than any of my friends."

"Bird watching could be your subject," Mrs. Grant offered. "Why don't you choose one bird to blog about today?"

"Bo?" Bridget asked, "have you ever heard of a catbird?"

"No," replied Bo. "Is it a cat with wings?"

"It's a songbird. It sounds like a cat. Meh, Meh," mewed Bridget.

Bo wanted to know more. "Where does it live?"

"Actually," Bridget thought aloud, "aside from here, I don't know."

"Then let's **research** it," said Mrs. Grant.

In a new Internet window, Mrs. Grant helped Bridget type the word catbird into a **search engine**. Bridget clicked one of the websites from the search results.

Bridget and Bo learned plenty about the grey catbird. They typed up their favorite details.

Grey catbirds live in the United States of America. They like to hide in forests and thick vines.

Grey catbirds are related to mockingbirds. Mockingbirds and catbirds can take songs from other birds to make their own special tune.

Bo chomped on a radish. "Before we start writing your blog, do you want to see some examples from other people's blogs?"

"Sure!" smiled Bridget.

11

"Here's an example of what not to do in a blog,"
said Bo. He opened a new website.

Guess Who's in Trouble

I know this girl whose name is Crystal Mason. She goes
to my school at Geoffrey Elementary School. She told me
something you all should know . . .

Bridget looked at Bo. "This is not going to be a very polite post."

"No," Bo shook his head. "We never say things in a blog that will hurt someone else's feelings. Can you see the other problem?"

Bridget read the page again, but she couldn't find an example.

13

"Look at this," said Bo, pointing to the name Crystal Mason. "Blogs are put online where everybody in the whole world can see. You shouldn't write people's full names."

"Very wise," applauded Mrs. Grant. "It's not safe to add private information like last names, addresses, or your school's name to blog posts."

"Why not?" asked Bridget.

"Most readers are trustworthy, safe people—like your friends and neighbors," explained Mrs. Grant. "But not everyone is that way. Always ask yourself: do I want a stranger to know this information? Trust your feelings. You can talk to your dad about it, too."

Bridget nodded. "Got it."

"Good!" replied Mrs. Grant, walking out of the room. "Now have fun!"

BO's BLOG

Afternoon Tea

When I was in England, I learned about teatime. Afternoon tea is more than just drinking tea. You also nibble scones with jam and cream while chatting with your friends. Sometimes you even get cucumber sandwiches with the crusts cut off. I like those!

You know what else I learned in England about having a cup of tea? You're not supposed to stick your fingers all the way through the handle of a teacup. You're supposed to pinch the handle to hold the cup. It's easy to spill the tea this way, so many people stick out a pinky finger. The pinky finger balances the cup—try it!

Bo **navigated** to his own blog. They read the most recent entry together. It was about afternoon tea in England.

"Is there anything else you want to know about blogging?" Bo asked.

"Well, does my blog have to be as long as yours?" asked Bridget.

"No, you can write as much or as little as you want," answered Bo.

Bridget scrunched her face. "Does blogging have any other rules?"

Bo said, "My mom said I should always think about my audience. Who's going to read my blog—my friends, my family, my teacher? What will be interesting for them to read?"

Bridget nodded. "So I should think about who's going to read my blog while I'm writing."

"Come on," said Bo. "Let's get away from the computer."

Out on the balcony, Bridget and Bo plopped into patio chairs.

Bo looked thoughtful. "Writing blogs is like being a news reporter. I'm the guy who reports on England. You report on birds. When we have some news to share, we blog about it so people will get the scoop."

"I like that idea!" said Bridget. "Hang on. Let me give this a try."

In her notebook, Bridget wrote an **introduction** for her blog post.

Today I visited my friend Bo. The grey catbird was one bird he had never heard of before. Maybe you would like to learn about this crazy bird, too.

"I like it!" said Bo.

"Thanks," said Bridget. "What's next?"

Bo answered, "I write my blogs like a story with a beginning, middle, and end."

Bridget returned to her notebook. She wrote furiously about the first time she saw a catbird. When finished, she looked up at Bo with a smile. "Can I read it to you? You too, Mrs. Grant?" she called through the window. Mrs. Grant came out to join them, and Bridget read out loud.

Grey catbirds are mysterious. The first time I ever saw one I was visiting a park with lots of trees and vines. I was walking along when I thought I heard a cat mew. I took out my binoculars, which were black until I added stars and glitter and purple puffy paint. I hoped I would see a mountain lion or a cute tabby cat, but I could only see a grey bird.

When she was done, Mrs. Grant and Bo applauded. "Great start!" said Mrs. Grant.

"Oh, but . . . look at the first paragraph," said Bo. "The main sentence says: Grey catbirds are mysterious. The stuff about decorating your binoculars is a different idea."

"But I liked that part!" exclaimed Bridget.

22

"You should save it then," Mrs. Grant encouraged. "Maybe tomorrow's blog will be all about your binoculars." Then she went back inside.

Together, Bo and Bridget revised her paragraph. They underlined sentences that belonged in a different story. "Great!" said Bo. "Let's go post it!"

"Wait!" exclaimed Bridget as she returned to her notebook. "I don't have a **conclusion** yet. Every story has to have an end."

She wrote furiously for a minute, then waved her notebook in the air. "Finished!" she called out. Then she and Bo flew back to the computer.

"Type it up!" Bo called, bouncing around the room while Bridget blogged.

"Mrs. Grant," called Bridget. "I'm ready to post my blog!"

Mrs. Grant joined them at the computer. She read Bridget's blog before it was posted. "This looks very good," she said. "I think it's time to post it!"

The little crowd cheered as Bridget's post appeared on screen. Bo read it aloud.

Today I visited my friend Bo. I asked him if he had ever heard of a grey catbird. He said no. Maybe you would like to learn about this crazy bird, too.

Grey catbirds are mysterious. The first time I ever saw one I was visiting a park with lots of trees and vines. I was walking along when I thought I heard a cat mew. With my binoculars I searched and searched the vines for a cat. I could only see a grey bird. I told my dad what had happened. He said I had spotted a grey catbird.

I had a lot of fun reading about grey catbirds with Bo this afternoon. We learned that these birds live in vines and forests all over America. Grey catbirds learn songs from other birds and then use them to make up new songs. Did you know grey catbirds can sing songs for up to ten minutes? Wow!

Mrs. Grant and Bo applauded. "Great job!" exclaimed Mrs. Grant. "But what are you going to call your post?"

"Call it 'Bo Is Great!'" Bo said, laughing.

Bridget laughed, too. "Yeah, right, Bo! Hey, how do I add a title?"

Bo taught Bridget to change her post by clicking the edit button. Bridget typed in her title: *The Crazy Catbird, My First Post Ever!!!*

"This is fun!" exclaimed Bridget. "Let's write another blog post!"

You Can Build a Blog, too!

Blogs are typed on the computer and posted online, but great bloggers keep a notebook, too. Have a notebook and pencil of your own. Take it with you wherever you go so you can write down stories as they happen.

Create a blog. Ask a parent or teacher to help you sign up for a blog website. Once you are signed up, you can choose a template, name your blog, and start writing!

Choose a subject you love. Focus on a subject that excites you and makes you want to learn more. Maybe a hobby, sport, things you see or read, or other activities you like. Think about who's going to read your blog and what they might like to read about. Ask a parent or a teacher to help you find your subject if you get stuck.

Tell one story at a time. Each time you blog, you will be sharing one story or bit of news about your subject. Bridget tells us about only one bird encounter at a time. What is one story you can tell us about your subject?

Do some research. Blogging is never boring when you learn new things. Check out a book from the library, a magazine, or browse online. Share the best web links and the titles of your favorite reference books.

Put it together. Write a final draft. Remember to have an introduction, a body, and a conclusion, or a beginning, middle, and end.

Revise. Can you cross out any words or ideas that are not supported by the main sentence of each paragraph? Save the leftovers for another blog post.

Publish. Type your work into your blog. Have an adult double-check your writing and make sure you are not revealing too much private information. Most blog websites allow you to send invitations to your friends. Send invites so your friends know your post is ready!

Read other blogs. Writing your own blogs is only half of the fun. Make sure to read what your friends are writing, too. In the comments section, ask questions about each person's subject. If you notice that a friend has forgotten something—like a title—kindly let them know. You and your friends can help one another become skillful bloggers!

Glossary

conclusion: tells your readers what they just read, and leaves them thinking about what you wrote.

introduction: tells your readers what they are about to read.

navigated: moved between websites on the internet.

research: to search for facts and information that you don't already know.

search engine: a webpage such as Google or Yahoo that helps you find information on the World Wide Web.

template: a premade pattern or design for a website.

For More Information

Books

Mack, Jim. *Journals and Blogging*. Chicago: Raintree, 2009.

Websites

KidBlog.Org
http://kidblog.org/home.php
A free website without advertisements where you can build your own blog.

Kids Learn to Blog! Free Resources
http://kidslearntoblog.com/free-resources/
#FreeVideoBloggingLessons
Access many blog-related resources, including video tutorials on how to begin blogging.

National Geographic Kids: Blogs!
http://kidsblogs.nationalgeographic.com/blogs/
Read blogs by kids from all over the world. Post your comments, too.

About the Author

Amanda StJohn loves bird watching and mountain climbing. She speaks Spanish and would like to visit Spain someday. She says, "Building blogs is a blast!"